FANTASTICALLY FUNNY STORIES

D0413747

London Borough of Richmond Upon Thames	
CXXXX 001 126 867	
HM	0753411458
YR	
PETERS	Jun-05

KINGFISHER
An imprint of Kingfisher Publications Plc
New Penderel House, 283-288 High Holborn
London WC1V 7HZ
www.kingfisherpub.com

First published by Kingfisher 1994
This edition published by Kingfisher 2005
2 4 6 8 10 9 7 5 3 1

Text copyright © Michael Rosen 1988, 1994
Illustrations copyright © Mik Brown 1988, 1994
Cover illustration copyright © Martin Chatterton 2005

Some of the material in this edition was previously published
by Kingfisher Books in 1988 in *Silly Stories.*

All rights reserved. No part of this publication may be reproduced,
stored in a retrieval system or transmitted by any means electronic,
mechanical, photocopying or otherwise without the prior
permission of the publisher.

A CIP catalogue record for this book is available from the
British Library.

ISBN-13: 978 0 7534 1145 2
ISBN-10: 0 7534 1145 8

Printed in India
1TR/1204/THOM/(PICA)/90WO/C

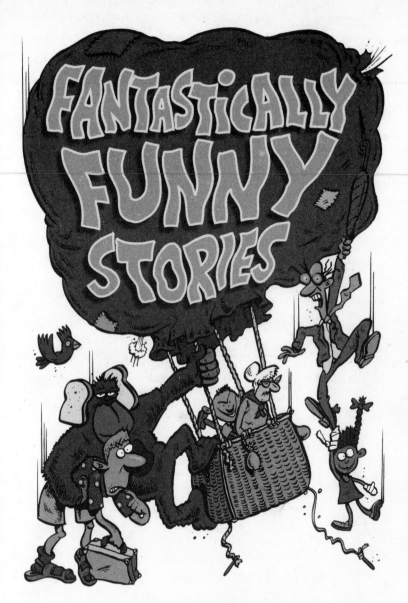

Michael Rosen
Illustrated by Mik Brown

KINGFISHER

Contents

Hands Off My Hankie!

A posh man was waiting at the doctor's. Opposite him was a small boy who kept sniffing.

Sniff-sniff. Sniff. SNIFF.

In the end, the man couldn't stand it any more.

"Have you got a hankie?" he said.
"Yeah," said the boy, "but I ain't lending it to you."

Wizard Slide

There were these three children and they came to a magic slide. A little man was standing there and he said, "Whatever you shout as you're sliding down this slide you get as a present when you get to the bottom."

So the first kid slides down and he shouts, "GOLD" and he lands up in a great big pile of gold.

The second kid slides down and he shouts, "DIAMONDS" and he lands up in a great big pile of diamonds.

And the third kid slides down and he shouts, "W H E E E E E" and he lands in a great big pool of . . . !

Thank Goodness!

There was this man, and he bought a horse, and he jumped on it and said, "GIDDYUP!" But the horse wouldn't move. So he said, "How do you make this horse go?"

And the man selling the horse said, "You say, 'Thank goodness'."

"And how do you get it to stop?" asked the man.

And the man selling the horse said, "You say, 'Belly button'."

So off went the man on the horse.

But the horse started going faster and faster, and the man started getting scared because he knew where the horse was taking him – right up to the edge of a Huge Cliff!

"Oh no," he thought, "I've forgotten how to get the horse to stop. What am I supposed to say? Oooooh, what is it?"

And the horse was getting nearer and nearer . . .

"What's the word? Oh, no . . . " And the horse was right up to the edge . . . and he remembered.

He shouted, "BELLY-BUTTON!" And the horse stopped.

"Phew," said the man. "Thank goodness." And the horse went whoooosh, straight over the edge.

Killer Cleaner

A boy went into a shop and said, "Can I have some cleaning fluid?"

The woman in the shop said, "Do you want a cleaner to put down the toilet, one that kills germs?"

The boy said, "Yes."

So the woman said, "I've got one here that kills very nearly all household germs." And she handed it to the boy.

It was in a bottle and next to it, stuck on with sellotape, was a great big hammer. So the boy said, "What's the hammer for?"

And the woman replied, "Well, I said that this cleaner kills nearly all household germs. The hammer is so that you can hit the last few on the head."

Double Trouble

Dave and Michael were watching a western.

As the hero, Sharpshooter Sam, rode into town, Michael said, "I bet you he falls off his horse."

Dave said, "Don't be a wally; Sharpshooter never falls off his horse."

"I bet you he falls off his horse in this film." said Michael.

"I bet you 50p he doesn't," said Dave.

They watched the film for a bit longer. Suddenly, some guns went off, Sharpshooter's horse reared up and Sharpshooter fell off his horse.

"See, I told you he would," said Michael.

"Oh, all right," said Dave. "Here's your 50p."

Michael hesitated. "No, I can't take your money," he said. "I've seen the film on video before."

"So have I," said Dave, "but I didn't think he'd be stupid enough to fall off again."

17

Excuses, Excuses!

There was a phone call for the head teacher, so she picked up the phone and said, "Yes?"

And a voice said, "I'm terribly sorry, Darren Wilkins won't be at school today."

So the headmistress said, "Why not?"

And the voice said, "'Cos he's ill in bed."

So the headmistress said, "Oh dear, what a shame, and who's speaking please?"

And the voice said, "My dad."

Water, Water, Water!

A man was going along in the desert in Australia when his car suddenly stopped. Nothing he could do would get it to go, so he got out and started to walk. He walked and he walked and he walked and soon he was feeling terribly, terribly thirsty. Finally he saw, coming into view, a little old shack by the side of the road. He staggered up to the door and shouted, "Water, water, water."

A man popped his head out the window and said, "Sorry pal, I only sell ties."

So the man walked on. And he walked and he walked and he walked.

By now his mouth was completely dried up. Then, coming into view, he saw another little old shack by the side of the road. He staggered up to the door and shouted, "Water, water, water."

A man popped his head out the window and said, "Sorry pal, I only sell ties."

So the man walked on.

Finally he couldn't walk any more, so he crawled. He crawled and he crawled and he crawled till, coming into view, he saw an hotel. There by the side of the road, right in the middle of the desert, was the Hotel Splendid. And a really splendid hotel it was, with a man in uniform standing on the steps outside.

The man crawled up to the steps and gasped, "At last. Water, water, water."

And the man in uniform said, "Sorry pal, you can't come in here dressed like that. You're not wearing a tie."

Medical Marvel

A little girl hurt her hand when she
fell over on her roller-skates, so she
went to see the doctor.

"Do you think I'll ever be able to
play the piano?" she said.

"Oh yes, dear," said the doctor
kindly, "you'll be able to play the
piano in just a few weeks' time."

"That's amazing," said the little
girl, "because I couldn't play before."

Mousetrap

A teacher asked her class if anything funny had happened to them that week. One girl told this story:

"We have mice at home and our cat is too lazy to catch them. Yesterday my Mum was late for work because there were three mice in the kitchen.

"She dashed out the house and, on the way to the station, she rushed in to a shop that sells mousetraps. 'Quick, I need a trap,' she said. 'Please hurry, I've got to catch a train.'

"And the man in the shop said, 'Sorry, madam, we haven't got any mousetraps that big.'"

Duck!

"Mum, Mum," shouted Tom, "Little 'Ally's broken my toy train."

"Now that's naughty, Sally," said Mum. "How did she do it, Tom?"

"She didn't duck when I hit her on the head with it," said Tom.

Pig!

The doctor called round at Mr Griffiths the farmer's house. Rosie, his little girl, opened the door.

"Is your father in?" asked the doctor.

"No," said Rosie.

"Will he be back soon?" asked the doctor.

"Oh, yes," said Rosie, "he's only in the pigsty, cleaning the pigs out. You'll see which one is Father—he's got his hat on."

Fashion Victim

Two young men who wanted to look
smart for going up to town were
checking each other's clothes over.

One of them says to the other,
"Your coat looks a right mess, you
ought to use a coat-hanger."

The next week when they met up,
the one who had been wearing the
untidy coat said, "I bought one of
those coat-hangers, but they don't half
make your shoulders ache."

Mistaken Identity

There was this group of people standing around with their dogs when along came a little man with a funny-looking yellow creature on a lead.

There was another man there with a great big alsatian dog, and just for fun, he let the alsatian off his lead and sent if off to scare the little man and his funny-looking yellow animal.

Just as the big alsatian came up to the funny-looking yellow animal, it lifted up its yellow head and, with one great big bite, bit off the alsatian dog's head.

The man who owned the alsatian said, "Oh no, what have you done? What sort of dog have you got there?"

The little man looked a bit sorry and
said, "Well, actually it's not
a dog. It's an alligator
with its tail
chopped off. I
painted it
yellow for
a joke."

Double Saving

A really mean man fell into the canal.
Luckily for him, a young man was
walking by who dived in and pulled
him out.

"Thank you very much, young
man," said the miser. "You've saved
my life and I would like to reward
you."

He put his hand into his pocket
and drew out a ten pound note.

"Oh," he said, "I would have
given you five pounds, but I'm afraid
all I've got is a ten pound note. I'm very
sorry." And he turned to go.

"That's easily put right," said the
young man. "Just jump in again and
I'll save you a second time."

Race Against Time

Dad was leaving to go to America. He had four minutes to catch his train to the airport. His family were all standing on the pavement saying goodbye to him when, suddenly, he realized he couldn't find his air-ticket.

So he said to his son, "Dash back to the flat and see if I left the ticket up there."

The family lived on the tenth floor . . . and the lift wasn't working. The son dashed off. Three minutes later he was back, panting like he'd run a marathon.

"Yes, Dad," he said, "your ticket's on the table, right where you left it."

Are You Being Served?

A man was sitting in a café having a drink when he called the waitress over. He pointed to his cup.

"This stuff tastes funny. What do you call it? Coffee or tea?"

"What do you mean, sir?" said the waitress.

"It tastes like paint," said the man.

"Ah, well," said the waitress. "If it tastes like paint, it must be coffee. Our tea tastes like soap."

Pencil
Puzzle

Everyone was in the classroom when the teacher said, "Where's your pencil, Maggie?"

"Ain't got one, miss," said Maggie.

And the teacher said, "How many times have I told you not to say, 'ain't got one.' Listen: I haven't got one. You haven't got one. They haven't got one. Now, do you understand?"

And Maggie said, "Well, where are all the pencils if nobody ain't got none?"

Intergalactic Nit-wit

There was this man who wanted to become an astronaut. So he went to the Space Center and did all kinds of tests. He thought he had done really well but, the day after the tests, he got a letter telling him he had failed.

"What went wrong?" asked his friend. "What did they ask you?"

"Well, the professor asked me, 'How will you know when you've reached the Moon?' So I said, 'There'll be a great big bump, sir.'

"Then the professor asked me 'What's the first thing you should

do when you reach the Moon?'
and I said, 'Try to get back.'

"Then they told me to check the
batteries. The professor said, 'I think
they're flat.' So I said, 'Yes, they are
very flat. What shape should they be?'

"After that we went up for a flight,
and the professor said, 'What is your
height and position?' So I replied, 'Five
foot ten, and I'm in the driver's seat.'

"And after all that, they didn't give
me the job!"

Gorilla Sandwich

A man went on holiday in Africa and bought a gorilla. On the way back he was coming through customs and he thought, "Oh no, I'm never going to be able to get through here; I know

you're not allowed to bring gorillas in.
I'll have to smuggle it in."

So what he did was slap a thick
slice of bread and butter on both ears
of the gorilla and he walked up to the
customs man.

The customs man went looking
through all his suitcases and bags and,
when at last he had finished, he looked
up and pointed at the gorilla.

"What's that?" he said.

The man got angry and said,
"Look here, of course you can go
through my suitcases, but what
I put in my sandwiches is
my business, OK?"

Animal Freshener!

A man went into a police station one day and said, "I want to complain. I've got three big brothers. We all live in one room. One of my brothers has got 17 cats. Another one has got 15 dogs. And the other one has got four goats and a pig. The smell in there is terrible. I want you to do something about it."

"Well, sir," said the policeman, "has the room got any windows?" "Yes, of course it has," said the man.

"Well, sir," said the policeman, "I suggest you open them."

"Don't be daft," said the man. "I'd lose all my pigeons."

Foot-loose!

Mrs Rossiter hadn't paid the electricity bill. She kept getting letters asking her to pay but she didn't reply. In the end, the electricity people sent a man over to cut off the electricity. Mrs Rossiter saw him coming and rushed off to hide

behind the curtain. Her son Mike
answered the door.

"Where's your mother?" said the
electricity man.

"She's out," said Mike.

"Oh, is she?" said the man,
looking at the bottom of the curtain.
"Does she always go out without her
feet on?"

Jumbo Jewel Thief

A boy was coming out of school when suddenly he saw an elephant. It walked up to a jeweller's shop on the corner, smashed the window and started sucking jewels up its trunk. After it had taken all the rings, gold watches and bracelets, it turned round and made off in the direction of the zoo.

The boy, who was called Joe, rushed off to the police station to tell them what he'd seen. A policeman took down everything that Joe told him and then said, "Now, lad, was this an African or an Indian elephant?"

"I don't know where it came from," said Joe.

"Well, lad," said the policeman, "the African elephant has big ears and the Indian elephant has small ears. What size ears did this one have?"

"I don't know, sir," said Joe. "It had a stocking over its head."

Dental Disaster

A woman went to the dentist for a check-up. The dentist had really bad eyesight.

When the dentist had finished, he said, "Thank you very much, that's all for now, Mrs Johnson."

And the woman said, "My name's not Johnson, it's Harvey. Remember, I'm Mrs Harvey, the one who came to see you about sore gums."

And the dentist said, "Sore gums? I'm not surprised you've got sore gums. I've just taken all your teeth out."

Ouch!

Class 6 were talking about television. They were having a discussion about violence on TV.

Hui-Lin said that violence was OK, so long as there wasn't too much of it.

James thought there shouldn't be any violence at all.

Then Maria said, "I used to like television, but all the violence has put me right off it. Every time I change channels, my brother hits me!"

Dad Lends A Hand

A girl was asking her dad a few things:

Haggies For Lunch

A man went to buy a car in London.

"Is this a good fast car?" he asked the salesman, pointing to a Super Whizzo Fast model.

"Fast?" replied the salesman. "Why, If you got in that car now, you could have your lunch in Scotland. Do you want to buy it?"

"I'll think about it," said the man, and he went home.

Next day he was back.

"I don't want that car," he told the salesman. "I lay awake all night thinking about it, but I couldn't think of a single reason why I'd want to have my lunch in Scotland."

Cat and Mouse

A man rang up the doctor in a terrible state.

"Doctor, my girlfriend was asleep in the armchair with her mouth open and a mouse ran into her mouth. What should I do?"

"Don't worry about it," said the doctor. "Just tie a lump of cheese on to a bit of string and put it in your girlfriend's mouth. When the mouse bites it, you can pull him out."

"Thank you, Doctor," said the man. "I'll dash round to the

supermarket now and get a tin of cat food before it shuts."

"Cat food?" said the doctor. "What do you want a tin of cat food for?"

"Oh," said the man, "I forgot to tell you . . . I've got to get the cat out first."

Whose book is this?

Michael Rosen wrote the words and Mik Brown drew the pictures. Here are some horribly silly facts about them.

Michael Rosen was born. When he was young he was a boy, though now he is a man. He's been collecting jokes and silly stories for

many years. He catches them with a large net and puts them in little cages on the window-sill and under the table. His house is now full of jokes and five of them are children. They collect jokes too, but most of them are too rude to mention.

Mik Brown first started illustrating jokes when he lived on a farm. His pigs, sheep, and chickens would tell them their funniest jokes and insist on posing for drawings. Mik can illustrate just about anything but he's not keen on drawing elephants. It's not that he doesn't like them or find their jokes funny, it's just that they take up too much room on his drawing board.

Other titles in the *Sidesplitters*
series you might enjoy: